HAIRSPRAY

The Novel

Adapted by Tracey West

Based on the Motion Picture
Screenplay by Leslie Dixon

Based on the 1988 Screenplay "HAIRSPRAY" written by John Waters,
and the 2002 Musical Stage Play "HAIRSPRAY,"
Book by Mark O'Donnell, Thomas Meehan,
Music by Marc Shaiman,
Lyrics by Scott Wittman, Marc Shaiman

PSS!
PRICE STERN SLOAN

PRICE STERN SLOAN
Published by the Penguin Group
Penguin Group (USA) Inc., 375 Hudson Street, New York, New York 10014, USA
Penguin Group (Canada), 90 Eglinton Avenue East, Suite 700, Toronto, Ontario M4P 2Y3,
Canada (a division of Pearson Penguin Canada Inc.)
Penguin Books Ltd., 80 Strand, London WC2R 0RL, England
Penguin Group Ireland, 25 St. Stephen's Green, Dublin 2, Ireland
(a division of Penguin Books Ltd.)
Penguin Group (Australia), 250 Camberwell Road, Camberwell, Victoria 3124, Australia
(a division of Pearson Australia Group Pty. Ltd.)
Penguin Books India Pvt. Ltd., 11 Community Centre, Panchsheel Park,
New Delhi—110 017, India
Penguin Group (NZ), 67 Apollo Drive, Rosedale, North Shore 0745, Auckland, New Zealand
(a division of Pearson New Zealand Ltd.)
Penguin Books (South Africa) (Pty.) Ltd., 24 Sturdee Avenue,
Rosebank, Johannesburg 2196, South Africa

Penguin Books Ltd., Registered Offices: 80 Strand, London WC2R 0RL, England

Published by Price Stern Sloan, a division of Penguin Young Readers Group,
345 Hudson Street, New York, New York 10014.
PSS! is a registered trademark of Penguin Group (USA) Inc. Printed in the U.S.A.

Library of Congress Control Number: 2007006611

ISBN 978-0-8431-2690-7   10 9 8 7 6 5 4 3 2 1

1

Hssssss . . . Hsssssss . . . Hsssssss . . .

A cloud of hairspray filled Tracy Turnblad's tiny bedroom. Tracy sprayed and sprayed until she couldn't see anything through the thick mist.

All of the coolest girls in 1962 wore their hair piled high. It took a minor miracle to keep all of that hair in place. Luckily, the miracle could be purchased in any beauty shop: Ultra-Clutch Hairspray.

The fog vanished, and Tracy looked at herself in the mirror. Her brunette 'do crowned her head like a hair helmet. Tracy grinned. You needed big hair when you were a big girl, and her hair was perfect. But just in case . . .

Hssssss . . . Hssssss . . . Hsssssss . . . .

Tracy finally put down the can. She ran out of her apartment and down the stairs. If she didn't hurry, she'd miss the school bus.

Tracy stepped out into the Baltimore sunshine. She walked past the window of her dad's joke shop, the Hardy Har Hut. As she walked, the rhythm of the city streets put a skip in her step.

"Good morning, Baltimore!" Tracy sang out joyfully. Every sound she heard was part of the bouncy melody running through her head. The rumble of the garbage trucks driving down the street. The pitter-patter of rats in the gutter. The couple arguing on their front stoop. The sounds made her hips sway and her fingers snap.

Tracy couldn't explain it, exactly. Lately a crazy energy had been bubbling up inside of her. The feeling made her want to dance—and she was good at it. Tracy dreamed of dancing in front of the world one day. She knew she could do it. And she wasn't going to let anyone stop her.

A song burst from Tracy as she danced down the street toward the waiting school bus.

"Something inside me makes me move when I hear the groove," Tracy sang. *"My ma tells me no, but my feet tell me go! It's like a drummer inside my heart . . ."*

Tracy got so carried away by her song that she forgot to get on the bus. She watched as it pulled away without her—she just couldn't be late for school again!

As another garbage truck rumbled past, Tracy got a wonderful idea. She grabbed onto the truck's ladder and hopped on. From her perch, Tracy felt like queen of the city. She belted out her song as the truck sped through the streets.

"*I love you, Baltimore!*" she sang. "*Every day's like an open door. Every night's like a fantasy. Every sound's like a symphony. And I promise, Baltimore, that someday when I take to the floor, the world's gonna wake up and see—Baltimore and me!*"

The garbage truck pulled in front of the school right behind the school bus. Tracy climbed down and ran through the doors just as the school bell rang. She had made it!

But Tracy's bubbly mood didn't last long. School was not exactly her favorite place. The only good thing about school was that Tracy had most of her classes with her best friend, Penny Pingleton. Penny's

mother was incredibly strict; she made Penny wear itchy wool jumpers and sensible loafers. And Mrs. Pingleton certainly didn't let Penny tease her hair as high as Tracy did! But Tracy thought her friend's blond ponytails were still pretty cool.

Tracy and Penny sat next to each other in history class. Their teacher, Miss Wimsey, was droning on and on again.

"Mount Everest is the most famous, but not the highest, geographical point on the earth," the teacher said. "Who can tell me what the highest point is?"

The boy sitting behind Tracy pointed at her hair. The kids in class giggled. Penny winced. Not everybody thought Tracy's super-high hair was cool.

The boy raised his hand. "Miss Wimsey, I can't see again," he complained.

The teacher frowned. "Miss Turnblad, if I have to write you up for inappropriate hair height one more time, you'll be removed to detention!"

"Miss Wimsey, what am I supposed to do?" Tracy protested. "Hair can't just hang like a dead thing on your cheeks . . ."

Tracy trailed off as she slumped in her seat. Why bother explaining herself? Miss Wimsey would never understand. Her limp gray hair had never been bathed in a beautiful cloud of hairspray.

The rest of the day dragged on . . . and on . . . and on. Tracy sat through science class, algebra class, and English class, but she didn't absorb a word she heard.

Instead, a song was running through her head. She couldn't bear sitting still for one moment longer. She wanted to dance.

Tracy kept looking at the clock. The minutes ticked by slowly. 2:57 . . . 2:58 . . . 2:59. And then, finally . . .

The bell rang. Every kid in school ran through the halls and headed for the exit. Tracy and Penny tried to make their way through the thick crowd.

"Push! We're late!" Tracy yelled.

Penny politely tapped the kid in front of her on the shoulder, but Penny was just too skinny to get through. This task needed a gal with some meat on her bones.

Tracy barreled into the crowd like a linebacker, pulling Penny behind her. They ran and got on the very first bus.

The bus dropped them a few blocks away from Tracy's house. They raced down the streets. Tracy wasn't dancing this time. She was on a mission.

Tracy and Penny ran past a TV store. A voice called out from a television set in the window. Tracy and Penny skidded to a stop. A gorgeous guy smiled from the screen.

"Hey there, teenage Baltimore! Don't change that channel! It's time for *The Corny Collins Show*!"

Tracy grabbed Penny's arm.

"Hurry!" she cried. "We're missing it!"

2

Tracy and Penny ran past the window of the Hardy Har Hut. Wilbur Turnblad was showing a customer how to juggle.

"Hi, Dad!" Tracy called.

"Hi, Mr. Turnblad!" added Penny.

Tracy's dad smiled and waved at the girls. They opened the door of the apartment building and rushed up the stairs.

"Come on, Penny!" Tracy urged.

"My mother says I'm not allowed to perspire!" Penny panted.

The girls burst into the Turnblad living room and Tracy lunged for the TV. When she turned it on, Corny Collins smiled from the black-and-white screen.

"*The Corny Collins Show* is brought to you by Ultra-Clutch Hairspray," he announced. "For hair that holds up even in a NASA wind tunnel!"

Tracy and Penny stared at the television set like two zombies. *The Corny Collins Show* was the absolute best show on TV, ever. Corny played all the newest music while teen boys and girls danced along to the tunes. The members of the dance council were the best in Baltimore. They knew all the latest dances— the Twist, the Pony, the Locomotion, and even the Mashed Potato.

The dancers all looked fabulous, too. The girls wore party dresses and the boys wore neatly pressed slacks and shirts. They bopped around Corny as he sang the show's theme song.

> *"Oh every afternoon you turn your TV on,*
> *And we know you turn the sound up when*
> *your parents are gone.*
> *And then you twist and shout for your*
> *favorite star.*
> *And once you've practiced every step that's*
> *in your repertoire,*
> *You better come on down and meet the*
> *nicest kids in town!"*

The dancers posed for the camera one at a time.

"I'm Amber!" said a girl with blond hair and a perfect smile.

"Brad!"

"Tammy!"

"Fender!"

"Shelley!"

"I.Q.!"

"Lou Ann!"

Tracy tapped her foot impatiently. Where was he? She had to see him. Those big, blue eyes. That dark, slicked-back hair. Finally, he danced up to the camera.

"And I'm Link!"

"*Aaaaaaaaaaah!*" Tracy and Penny screamed. Link Larkin was the cutest guy in their school—and on the whole planet!

Corny grinned and finished the song.

> "*Who cares about sleep when you can snooze in school?*
> *They'll never get to college but they look so cool.*
> *Who needs a cap and gown, 'cause they're the nicest kids in town!*"

"Would you keep that racket down?" a grouchy voice boomed from the next room.

Edna Turnblad, Tracy's large and formidable mother, stomped into the living room. Her hands were planted firmly on the hips of her flowered housecoat and she glared at the girls from behind a strand of limp brown hair.

"I'm trying to iron here!" Edna snapped. She pointed to the tiny room behind her, which was filled with an ironing board and baskets full of clothes.

"Ma, it's not a racket!" Tracy answered, her eyes never leaving the TV screen. "It's *The Corny Collins Show*!"

Edna moved to the TV and turned down the volume.

"It's turning your brains to mud," she said.

"Oh please, Mrs. Turnblad. It's a new dance!" Penny begged.

"The Stricken Chicken!" Tracy wailed.

Edna walked back to her iron, muttering, "Can't hear myself think. Just how am I supposed to negotiate pleats?"

10

Just then, a thin, uptight-looking woman with mousy brown hair appeared in the entryway. It was Prudy Pingleton, Penny's mom.

Penny immediately dove behind the couch, but Tracy didn't notice a thing. She was busy copying the steps of the Stricken Chicken.

Prudy crossed over to Edna's ironing room. "Edna, is my laundry ready?" she asked.

"That'll be three dollars," Edna replied.

Prudy frowned. "That's pretty pricey for a pair of pettipants," she said sourly. She looked into the living room and frowned. "You're letting her listen to that race music again? My daughter spends every afternoon at the Stamp and Coin Club."

Edna raised an eyebrow in surprise. "What? Prudy, your daughter's right—"

Tracy frantically waved her arms to try to stop her mother from talking. If Penny's mom knew she was watching *The Corny Collins Show*, Penny would be in big trouble!

Edna saw Tracy and thought her daughter was still dancing along with the show. "What's that one called,

11

the Wavin' Raven? It's a little twitchy," Edna said.

Tracy shook her head. She pointed to Penny behind the couch. Finally, Edna figured it out—and she wasn't happy.

"Tracy Turnblad, are you telling me that Penny doesn't have her mother's permission to be here?" she bellowed.

Prudy glared at Tracy. Penny slowly emerged from behind the couch—she knew she was trapped.

"No Corny Collins for a week!" Edna told Tracy as she turned off the TV.

Penny's mom dragged her out of the apartment.

"You are banned from that house, and you are never watching that TV show again!" she fumed.

"No . . . please, mother. Without that show I have nothing!" Penny pleaded.

"Having nothing builds character," Prudy said firmly.

Tracy sank into the couch, miserable. Penny was in big trouble. And now she couldn't watch Corny Collins for a whole week!

How was she going to survive?

3

Over at the TV station, the dancers were moving to a new tune.

Link was dancing with a pretty blonde named Amber Von Tussle. She took the lead and danced directly in front of all the other dancers. Amber loved getting camera time.

A dancer named Lou Ann was the only thing between Amber and the camera now. Amber gave Lou Ann a little shove. The brown-haired girl didn't budge.

Amber scowled and used her elbow to jab Lou Ann in the ribs. Lou Ann groaned and moved to the side. Amber grinned triumphantly for the camera.

"We'll be right back, with some of that hot Detroit sound!" Corny announced when the song ended.

The camera light shut off as the show went to commercial.

Velma Von Tussle, Amber's mother, rushed up

to Corny. She wore a slinky dress and a scowl on her face.

"Detroit sound?" Velma complained. "What's that—the cries of people being mugged?"

Besides her 1962 hairdo, Velma had a 1962 attitude—a bad one. Velma thought black people and white people should be kept apart. She didn't like music by black performers, either. Most of that music was made in the Motown studio in Detroit, Michigan.

"Aw, Velma, the kids really dig rhythm and blues," Corny said, trying to wave her aside.

"They're kids, Corny," Velma said. "That's why we have to steer them in the white direction."

"You mean the *right* direction," Corny corrected her.

Velma innocently batted the lashes of her big, blue eyes. "Didn't I say that?"

Corny frowned, but there wasn't much he could do. Besides being Amber's mom, Velma was the TV station manager.

Across the studio, Lou Ann lunged at Amber. I.Q. grabbed her and held her back.

Amber snarled at Lou Ann. "Next time you try that, there'll be stumps where your feet used to be, you—"

Just then, Link walked up and Amber was all smiles.

"Great dancing today, Lou Ann," she said brightly.

When Link gave Amber a hug and a kiss, Lou Ann rolled her eyes and walked away.

Velma stormed over to them.

"Stop that!" she said, pulling Link and Amber apart. "Amber, save your personal life for the camera."

"Speaking of which," Velma said, turning to the cameraman. "Did you have a nice nap? If you did your job better, my daughter wouldn't have to fight to be visible," Velma snapped.

"I gotta show some of the other kids once in a while," he argued.

Velma eyed the cameraman, sizing him up.

"This is a small city. Not that many TV stations," she said in an icy voice. "This time next week you could be wearing an ill-fitting tux, snapping bar mitzvah photos."

The cameraman gulped and nodded nervously,

readying his camera to film Amber as soon as the commercial ended.

Even though Tracy and Penny couldn't watch *The Corny Collins Show* at the Turnblads' anymore, they found a way. Luckily for them, the TV stores downtown kept television sets in the windows. At four o'clock every day, most of them were set to Corny Collins.

The girls watched the show through the shop window. Link was singing a song, but the camera was focused on Amber the entire time.

"Why won't they show Link?" Tracy cried. "This is nuts. She can't even dance!"

"Plastic little spastic," Penny agreed.

Finally, the camera showed Link singing. Tracy sighed and pressed her hands against the glass.

"Oh Link, I can dance so much better than she can," Tracy said. "If only you knew."

The song ended, and the camera turned to Corny. A black woman with a big smile and a big head of blond hair stood next to him.

"I'm Motormouth Maybelle, reminding you next

Tuesday's your rhythm and blues day. Negro Day will be coming your way!" she said.

Tracy nodded. The dancers on Negro Day were some of the best around. And the music was totally cool. Sometimes, though, she wondered why the black kids and white kids couldn't dance on the same show. It just didn't seem right.

"Owner's coming!" Penny cried suddenly. "He'll call my mother again. Let's go!"

Penny started to pull Tracy away, but something Corny was saying made them both stop.

"It's time to say good-bye to our little Brenda. She'll be leaving the show," Corny said. "So it seems we'll have an opening for a new girl on the council. Wanna be one of the nicest kids in town? Cut school tomorrow and come on down to station WYZT to audition!"

Tracy froze. Corny Collins needed a new girl dancer. She was a girl. She was a dancer. She was a girl dancer!

This was her chance to be famous!

Now all she had to do was get permission to get out of school for the audition.

17

Tracy asked her mom at dinner that night.

"No!" Tracy's mom replied.

"But *Maaa*!" Tracy wailed.

"Don't test me, Tracy Turnblad," Edna snapped. "My diet pill is wearing off."

"But—"

Edna frowned. "No one in this house is auditioning for anything!" she said firmly. She plopped a big scoop of mashed potatoes on Tracy's plate as if to finalize her point.

Tracy felt like crying. "But why not? Why not?"

Edna put her hands on her wide hips. "Tracy Turnblad, dancing is not your future. Sometime you'll own Edna's Occidental Laundry."

"I don't want to be a laundress," Tracy protested. "I want to be famous!"

"You want to be famous? Learn how to get blood out of car upholstery," Edna said proudly. "That's a skill you can take right to the bank!"

Tracy's father walked into the kitchen, looking concerned.

"Hey, what's all the ruckus in here?" Wilbur asked.

Tracy opened her mouth to answer him, but Edna stopped her with a look.

"Not. Another. Word," Edna hissed.

Wilbur sat down at the table. There was silence for a moment. Then . . .

"Daddy, tomorrow I'm auditioning to be on a TV show!" Tracy blurted out.

"You are?" Wilbur asked. He sounded excited.

"No she is not!" Edna insisted. "First the hair, now this!"

"Aw, hon, all the kids are battin' up their hair now," Wilbur said.

Tracy smiled. Maybe things weren't hopeless yet. "It's called ratting, Daddy, and our First Lady, Jacqueline Kennedy, does it," she told him.

"I don't believe that," Edna said.

"What do you mean, you don't believe it?" Tracy said. She turned to her dad. "Are you hearing this? How else would her hair look that way?"

"It's naturally stiff," Edna insisted.

Tracy jumped out of her seat.

"Mom doesn't understand anything!" Tracy cried.

"Now, don't disabuse your mother," Wilbur gently scolded.

"Dancing on that show is my dream!" Tracy said. She nodded toward her mother. "Just because she wouldn't know a dream if it bit her on the nose—"

Edna stood up. "For your information, missy, I once dreamed I'd own a coin-operated Laundromat. I came off that cloud pretty quickly, I can tell you!"

"*Aaaaaaaaaaah!*" Tracy screamed and stormed out of the room.

Edna sighed and sat back down. "She thinks I'm being mean," she told Wilbur. "I don't know how to tell her. They don't put girls like Tracy on TV . . . people like us . . ."

Edna couldn't bring herself to say the word "fat." But she knew other people used it. And a lot of those people weren't so nice.

"It's gonna hurt her, Wilbur," she said sadly.

Wilbur nodded.

"I'll talk to her," he said.

Wilbur went into Tracy's bedroom. She was

stretched out on her bed and had a miserable look on her face. Wilbur looked around the room at all the pictures and posters of singers and dancers on the walls. It was easy to see how much music meant to Tracy.

He sat down on the edge of the bed. "Tracy, this TV thing, you really want it?"

"With all my heart," Tracy said, wiping a tear from her cheek.

"Then you go for it!" Wilbur said, suddenly changing his tune. "This is America, babe. You gotta think big to be big!"

Edna stood in the doorway, furious.

"Being big is not the problem, Wilbur!" she said.

Wilbur took Tracy's hands in his. "You follow your dream, baby," he said. "Mine came true. And now I have . . . the most precious thing in the world."

Edna's angry look melted. Was Wilbur talking about her?

"I've got the Taj Mahal of joke shops!" Wilbur said as he walked to the door.

Edna scowled as she and Wilbur left Tracy alone.

Tracy sat up on her bed, grinning.

Once the people at the TV station saw her dance, they'd see how great she was.

Soon the whole world would know, too!

4

The next morning, Tracy and Penny stood outside the WYZT television station. They joined a line of other girls, all hoping to be picked to dance on *The Corny Collins Show*.

The council girls walked slowly down the line, led by Amber Von Tussle. They sized up each waiting girl one by one. When Amber got to Tracy, she stopped.

"The gym's next door," Amber said, with a nasty grin on her face.

"No, um, I'm here to audition," Tracy told her.

The girls snickered behind Amber. Just then, Link walked out of the studio door. He started signing autographs for girls in the line.

"I cut school to come down here," Tracy told the council girls. "Isn't that cool?"

Amber didn't seem impressed. But Link smiled and winked at Tracy.

"This is some sort of joke, right?" Amber asked. The girls giggled.

But Tracy had already tuned out Amber's words. Link Larkin had winked at her! Things were getting off to a great start already.

Soon the auditioning girls were ushered into the studio. Tracy and Penny watched as Velma Von Tussle drilled the council dancers in their steps.

"Front, step, cha-cha-cha. Back, step, cha-cha-cha. Side, step, front, step, back, and turn," Velma chanted.

The dancers lined up, boys facing girls, and copied the steps exactly. Tracy spotted Link dancing with Amber. She nudged Penny.

"Oh my gosh! There's Link! Link!" Tracy cried. "Penny, pinch me!"

Penny pinched Tracy's arm.

"Ow!"

Penny was confused. "But you told me to—"

But Tracy was gazing around the studio, thrilled. "I can't believe I'm really here auditioning!" she shrieked.

"I can't believe I'm really here watching you audition!" Penny shrieked back.

Velma glanced quickly at the auditioning girls.

"Amber, look at this motley crew," she told her daughter. "These girls must be deranged. Do they really think they've got what it takes to dance on TV?"

Amber wasn't listening. She started to groove to the music, doing her own thing.

"Amber! Stop wiggling your hips like that," Velma scolded.

Amber rolled her eyes. "Mother, wake up from that dream of yours. This isn't 1930."

"Don't tell me how to dance," Velma snapped. "I was voted Miss Baltimore Crabs in my day. I knew the right way to dance then, and I still do. Now go get those girls and let's get this over with!"

Amber and the council girls led the auditioning girls in front of Velma. Tracy tapped her foot nervously. This was her big chance!

"Good day, ladies," Velma said. "Let's see what you've got."

The dancers demonstrated a combination of moves.

"Twist, twist, twist, twist, mashed potato, mambo," the dancers sang.

Most of the girls in line struggled with the moves. But Tracy picked them up right away. She forgot about being nervous and concentrated on the rhythm.

She was doing great. She knew it. But there was more to the audition than dancing. Amber and Velma walked down the line, interviewing the girls.

Amber stopped in front of one girl.

"This one will never get a date in those hand-me-down clothes," she said.

"Kid, she'll never get a date till her Daddy buys her a new nose," Velma added.

The poor girl put her hand to her nose. She looked like she might cry.

They stepped in front of a girl standing right next to Tracy. The girl wore an ugly plaid shirt.

"Do you dance like you dress?" Amber asked.

Link appeared behind her. "Amber, there's no need to be cruel!"

Now it was Tracy's turn. Velma stared at her with cold blue eyes.

"Would you swim in an integrated pool?" she asked.

There was a hush in the studio. Tracy smiled. This was an easy question. Integration—blacks and whites going to the same schools, restaurants, and other places—was definitely the way to go, as far as she was concerned.

"I would!" Tracy said confidently. "I'm all for integration. It's the new frontier!"

A few people gasped. Velma's eyes narrowed.

"Not in Baltimore it isn't," she said. "And may I be frank? If your size weren't enough, your last answer just blew it. You'll never be in—so we're kicking you out!"

Velma pushed Tracy backward until she found herself near the door.

"You may go," Velma said.

"Um, thank you," Tracy answered. She didn't feel angry, or even sad. She was stunned.

As Tracy stood there, frozen, a young black girl

walked through the door. She looked very cute—and very nervous.

"Hello, ma'am," she said to Velma. "May I please audition?"

"No!" Velma said. Then she shut the door.

Penny put a hand on Tracy's shoulder.

"I could tell that they secretly liked you," she said, trying to be encouraging.

Tracy didn't say a thing. She felt empty inside, like a balloon with no air in it.

Her dream of dancing on *The Corny Collins Show* had just been dashed.

Maybe her mom was right after all!

5

Tracy tried to tiptoe quietly back into Miss Wimsey's class after her audition. When she slipped into her seat, the chair creaked loudly.

Miss Wimsey had her back to the class, but she didn't have to turn around. She knew exactly what that sound was.

"Cutting my class, Tracy Turnblad?" she asked. "I trust it was something really important."

Tracy sighed. "It should have been."

Miss Wimsey turned to her desk. She ripped a pink detention slip off of her desk. Tracy groaned. She had never been to detention before.

After school, Tracy reluctantly made her way to the school basement. She stopped in front of a door marked "Detention" and peeked inside.

A small transistor radio was playing music in the back of the room. A bunch of kids were lounging

around on some beat-up old desks. None of them looked happy to be there.

Tracy stepped inside and immediately noticed she was the only white kid in the room. In 1962 Baltimore, that didn't happen too often.

"What are you looking at?" one of the boys asked.

"Nothing," Tracy said quickly. "Not you."

She slid across the back wall, not sure what to do. "Um, I'm not sure I belong here," she said, a little nervously.

"Don't none of us do," said Seaweed, a thin boy. "You think we did anything to get sent down here?"

"This is where they keep us stashed!" added Stooey, the other boy.

Seaweed turned up the radio, and the kids began to dance. Tracy couldn't help staring. Their dancing was amazing and fresh. Nothing like the boring cha-cha Velma Von Tussle had been leading that morning.

"Can I help you?" asked Duane, a short boy with a scowl on his face.

"That move's swift," Tracy said.

Duane nodded. "You got that right."

Seaweed grinned. "The man can dine me on a diet of detention so long as he don't starve me of my tunes."

Tracy's body swayed to the beat as she watched him dance. "Does that dance have a name?"

"I call it 'Peyton Place After Midnight,'" Seaweed replied. "I use it to attract the ladies."

"Wow, that's unbelievable," Tracy said, watching his feet. "So . . . kind of like this?"

She tried to copy the dance.

"You can't do that dance!" Duane scoffed. "Look at her, Seaweed, thinkin' she can just—" He stopped. Tracy *could* do the dance. She could really move.

Seaweed grinned. "Not bad for a white chick."

As Tracy looked at Seaweed, she suddenly realized something.

"Hey!" she cried. "I've seen you before."

She and Seaweed fell in step, dancing together.

"Yeah, where?" Seaweed asked.

"On Corny's show. On Negro Day!" Tracy cried. "Negro Day is the best. I wish every day were Negro Day."

"At our house it is," Seaweed said with a grin.

"Show me another one?" Tracy asked.

Seaweed nodded. He broke into some funky moves, chanting while he danced.

"Here's a little something, something to say, 'Hello, my name's Seaweed J. Stubbs, and what's yours, baby?'"

Tracy responded with her own funky step. "And I'm Tracy Turnblad!"

Seaweed and Tracy laughed as they continued to dance together.

"Girl, you ain't just happening, you have happened!" Seaweed said, impressed.

Tracy nodded. "You're joining this show already in progress!"

Tracy was having so much fun dancing with Seaweed that she forgot she was in detention. Outside in the hallway, Link and I.Q. were walking by.

"Yeah, I get who Caesar was," I.Q. was saying. "But what's with the Ideas of March? I mean, how can a month have an idea?"

Link was about to explain things to I.Q. when he

heard music coming from the detention room. Curious, he looked inside and saw Tracy, Seaweed, and the other kids grooving to the music. Tracy and Seaweed were definitely the best dancers in the room.

"Come on," I.Q. said.

"Just a minute," Link replied, brushing him off. He wanted to see Tracy dance some more.

In the room, Seaweed smiled at Tracy. "So how you feeling about detention now?"

"You can lock me up and throw away the key!" Tracy said, grinning back at him.

When Link walked into the room, Tracy stopped in mid-step, stunned.

"Wha-wha-wha—" she babbled. She couldn't help it. The sight of Link's gorgeous grin made her brain turn to mush.

"You know, Corny's hosting the hop tomorrow," Link told her. "Maybe if he saw you dancing like that he'd put you on the show."

Tracy nodded, beaming. When the bell rang, all the kids in detention ran for the door. When Tracy and Link headed for the door, they bumped into each other.

Tracy froze. She had just touched Link Larkin! Link apologized and then walked away. Tracy stared after him like she was in a trance.

Penny ran in, grabbed Tracy's arm, and started talking. But Tracy didn't hear a word she said. There was so much she could have told Penny. She could have told her about Seaweed. Or about Corny hosting the hop in a few days. But she couldn't talk. There were bells ringing in her head. Bells that chimed along with the beating of her heart.

"Link," Tracy finally managed to mutter. "He talked to me. He even touched me."

She rubbed the arm that had accidentally bumped into Link.

"Oh Penny, I'm in love!" Tracy confessed to her friend. "I feel like I've been hit with a ton of bricks."

Penny just shook her head. She knew her friend had it bad for Link.

The bells in Tracy's head didn't stop ringing for days. Tracy thought of Link every moment of every day. When she practiced with her driver's ed instructor, she imagined she was driving around with Link. She saw Link's face on every dodgeball in gym class. And when Link was around she couldn't take her eyes off him. She watched Link's every move as he and his friends ate lunch. She even gazed at Link as he walked with his arm around Amber, his girlfriend.

Tracy didn't care. She knew she and Link were destined to be together. She wasn't hearing bells in her head for nothing.

Finally the night of the hop arrived. When Tracy and Penny entered the school gym, they saw Link dancing on a small platform at the end of the gym, singing a song. Corny watched the crowd, clapping along with Link. The other thing Tracy noticed was that a velvet rope divided the gym in half. Whites stayed on one side of the rope, and blacks stayed on the other.

"Go on, get out there where Corny can see you," Penny told Tracy.

Lots of kids had the same idea. It wouldn't be easy getting near Corny.

"Front row's packed pretty tight," Tracy said.

"I'll go up there and push," Penny suggested.

Tracy knew that wouldn't do much good. "Wait," she told her friend.

Tracy walked up to the velvet rope and found Seaweed dancing on the other side.

"Seaweed! Wanna do Peyton Place for Corny?" she called out.

Seaweed pointed at the rope. "You crazy? You gotta dance with your crowd and I gotta dance with mine."

"Why?" Tracy asked. That didn't make any sense to her at all.

"There's them, and then there's us. It's just the way it is," Seaweed said, shrugging.

"But it's *your* dance," Tracy said.

Seaweed waved his arm with a flourish. "Well then you just go and borrow it for a minute."

Tracy smiled in thanks. She started doing the Peyton Place, just like she and Seaweed had done in detention. She danced closer and closer to the front of the crowd. People were starting to step aside and take notice. Tracy was really tearing it up.

Amber noticed—and didn't like what she saw at all. She tried to trip Tracy, but Tracy saw it coming. She

36

stepped over Amber's foot, turning it into a cool dance move.

Finally Tracy made it to the front of the line.

Corny Collins stopped dead when he saw Tracy coming. The girl had rhythm. She had moves. And most of all, she could really dance.

A slow smile spread across Corny's face.

6

After school the next day, Penny Pingleton raced down the street. She stopped in front of the Hardy Har Hut and pressed her face against the glass.

"Mr. Turnblad! Come quick!" Penny called out.

Wilbur didn't ask any questions. He followed Penny upstairs to the Turnblad apartment. Just as Penny turned on the TV, the opening theme song to *The Corny Collins Show* began to play.

Penny dragged Edna away from her ironing board. "Hurry! You have to see this!"

Edna frowned when she saw the television. The dance council was smiling at the camera, just like they did every day.

"Darla!"

"Paulie!"

"Noreen!"

"Doreen!"

"Link!"

Then Tracy's beaming face appeared.

"And I'm . . . Tracy!" she cried.

"*Aaaaaaaaaaaaah!*" Penny, Wilbur, and Edna let out a wild shriek. Tracy was on TV!

"*So if every night you're shakin' as you lie in bed,*" Corny sang.

"Go, Tracy! Go, go, Tracy!" shouted Wilbur.

"*And the bass and drums are pounding in your head . . .*"

"Shake it, Tracy!" Edna yelled.

Penny, Edna, and Wilbur tried to copy the moves they saw on TV. They danced around the living room.

"*Who cares about sleep when you can snooze in school?*

They'll never get to college but they look so cool.

Who needs a cap and gown,

'cause they're the nicest kids in town!"

In the studio, Velma Von Tussle watched as the kids did a new dance. She was horrified. These weren't the neat little steps she had taught the dancers. Mr.

Spritzer, one of the show's sponsors, stood next to her. He looked just as upset.

"I don't know what happened, Mr. Spritzer," Velma said. "Corny had some sort of aneurysm and picked that new girl!"

"*They're the nicest kids in town!*" Corny crooned, and the song ended with a big finish.

"Yeah!" Corny cried. "And that was the dance of the week, Peyton Place at Midnight. Introduced to you by our brand-new council member, Miss Tracy Turnblad! So, Trace! Cozy up to old Corny and tell us about yourself!"

"Well, I watch *The Corny Collins Show*," Tracy replied eagerly. "And I do absolutely nothing else!"

Back in the Turnblad living room, Edna wiped a tear from her eye. "Oh, Wilbur. To think I almost stopped her from reaching for the stars."

"And now here she is on local daytime TV!" Wilbur said proudly.

They watched to see what Tracy would say next.

"I also hope to be the first woman president," Tracy told Corny. "Or a Rockette."

"And if you were president, what would your first act be?" Corny asked her.

Tracy looked right into the camera and gave a big smile. "I'd make every day Negro Day!"

Backstage, Velma and Mr. Spritzer screamed in horror.

In the control room, telephones began to light up.

Corny nodded his head in agreement with Tracy. "I read you like tomorrow's headlines, Trace! What do you say, kids? Looks like we might have a hot new candidate for Miss Teenage Hairspray!"

"That's only the dream of my life!" Tracy added.

Corny looked at the camera. "And that dream will be coming to you live, Saturday, June sixth, right here at WYZT!"

Amber stomped her foot. "No! Miss Hairspray's mine!"

"We're on the air," Link hissed. But Amber ignored him.

"They can't! They have to vote for a person, not one of the Himalayas," Amber said meanly.

Velma noticed that the cameraman was getting a

close-up of Amber's hissy fit. She waved her arms at Amber in warning.

"If you think—" Amber began. Then she noticed her mother. A fake smile immediately appeared on her face. " . . . that I'm not thrilled to have this new member in our council family, then you're wrong!"

Amber leaned in and gave Tracy an insincere hug.

"And we're off the air!" Velma yelled. She glared at the cameraman. He shrugged.

"You said to give Amber a close-up whenever possible," he said, smiling.

After the show ended, Velma called Corny into her office. Mr. Spritzer launched into a screaming fit.

"I want that chubby, communist girl off the show!" Mr. Spritzer fumed.

"Well, let me be the first to toss the harpoon," Velma chimed in.

"Now hold on—" Corny said angrily.

Mr. Spritzer pounded his fist on Velma's desk. "She's a corrupting influence!"

"I agree," Velma said. "We don't want our dancers thrusting like savages."

Corny frowned. "Hey now, speak for yourself."

"Don't you be flip with me," Velma snapped.

"I'm not," Corny said. "I've got a few new ideas for updating the show. First, get rid of Negro Day—"

"Finally! Some sense out of you," Velma said.

"And mix those kids in with the council members," Corny finished.

Velma and Mr. Spritzer's mouths fell open.

"Mix those kids?" Mr. Spritzer asked in disbelief.

"This show isn't a black-and-white cookie," Velma said.

"Why couldn't it be?" Corny shot back. "Come on, Velma. Isn't this where it's all heading? You can fight it, or you can rock out to it."

Corny and Velma stared at each other for a moment. Neither one wanted to back down.

"Maybe it is time for some fresh ideas," Velma finally said in a sweet voice. "Like a nice, fresh, new host!"

The threat didn't phase Corny. "Gee, Velm, how do you fire Corny Collins from *The Corny Collins Show*?"

Corny walked out of the office.

"They do it all the time on *Lassie!*" Velma called after him.

Mr. Spritzer walked up to Velma, shaking his head. "Velma, you've let this go too far. Fix it."

As he walked away, Velma looked out into the studio and glared at Tracy. She was teaching more of those uncivilized dance moves to the council.

Mr. Spritzer, who owned Ultra-Clutch Hairspray, was one of the show's biggest sponsors. He wanted her to fix things? That would be easy.

All she had to do was get Tracy Turnblad off of the council!

7

Tracy became an instant celebrity in Baltimore. Everyone recognized her from *The Corny Collins Show*.

People started calling the TV station, voting for Tracy to be crowned Miss Teenage Hairspray. She almost had as many votes as Amber!

At the Turnblad apartment, the phone rang off the hook. People wanted Tracy to do everything from judging bake-offs to kissing their brand-new babies.

Wilbur got right into the spirit of things. He started selling Tracy souvenirs in the Hardy Har Hut. For a few bucks, Tracy fans could buy a signed photo or an official Tracy Turnblad wig.

Tracy had never been popular in high school. But now, everyone wanted to be her friend.

The detention room became the hippest place in school. Kids got in trouble just so they could hang

out there. They crowded in front of the door, waving their detention slips. Stooey kept watch at the door. He wanted to make sure only the coolest kids got in.

One afternoon when Stooey peeked out the detention room door, he saw Penny Pingleton's face staring back at him.

Stooey rolled his eyes. Penny was definitely *not* cool.

Luckily, Tracy was right there and opened the door for Penny. Stooey eyed Penny suspiciously.

"Where's her write-up?" he asked.

"She doesn't need one," Tracy said. "She's with me."

That was good enough for Stooey. He nodded and let her step inside. As Penny looked around the room, her eyes met Seaweed's eyes. When Seaweed smiled at Penny, she shyly looked at the floor.

Tracy had never been happier in her whole life. But not everyone was happy for Tracy.

Amber didn't like being upstaged by Tracy on the show. She didn't want Tracy to become Miss Teenage Hairspray. And she *definitely* didn't like the way Link looked at Tracy.

Velma didn't like Tracy's message. She did not want *The Corny Collins Show* to be integrated. But the more Tracy talked about it, the more other people seemed to want it, too.

Amber had a hard time keeping her feelings about Tracy to herself. One day on the show, Amber, Tammy, and Shelley sang "The New Girl in Town," a brand-new hit by the Dynamites, an all-black girl group.

"You better tell the homecoming queen to hold on to her crown, or she's gonna lose it to the new girl in town. She's hip, so cool . . ." the girls sang.

"I'm gonna get her after school!" Amber blurted out, changing the words.

Later in the week, on Negro Day, the Dynamites sang the song the right way.

"This town's in a stew, girl.
What a hullabaloo, girl!
She ain't just passing through, girl.
She's sticking like glue, girl,
To the man I thought I knew, girl.
Wo-oo, wo-oo, wo-oo, wo-oo!"

The host, Motormouth Maybelle, danced along as the Dynamites sang. When the three singers finished, all the dancers came out onstage with Maybelle, including Seaweed.

"Now that's the way it's done!" Maybelle said, looking into the camera. "And I'm the fabled Miss Motormouth Maybelle! Your DJ du jour, pitchin' rhythm your way! So hey, better shimmy and sway, we'll be back with some more of Negro Day!"

The lights of the camera faded.

"And thank God, we're off!" Velma said. "How dare you pick the same song that my Amber sang?"

Maybelle nodded to the Dynamites. "They wrote it."

Velma opened her mouth, then closed it. She couldn't argue with that.

"You just watch yourself," she warned. "You are one inch away from being canceled."

Velma spun around on her high heels and left. Seaweed glared after her and Maybelle put an arm around his shoulder.

"Foot in the door, that's all it is. One toe at a time," said Maybelle. Then she smiled and looked in Velma's

direction. "Something's eating her worse than usual."

Velma stomped down the hallway and paused in front of the council girls' dressing room. There was a sack of fan mail on Tracy's double-wide director's chair and several vases filled with flowers on Tracy's makeup stand.

The only mail that Amber had gotten that day was a flyer for pimple cream.

If that weren't bad enough, Mr. Spritzer walked in, smiling and waving a piece of paper.

"Look at this! That big little girl's sent my hairspray sales through the roof!" he told Velma happily.

Just then, Tracy walked by the door with two of the council girls. They both had hair just like Tracy's now. Everyone wanted a hairdo like Tracy's—and that was good news for Mr. Spritzer.

"People out there are breathing more aerosol than oxygen!" he said.

Velma sighed.

Getting rid of Tracy Turnblad was going to be harder than she thought!

8

That same afternoon, the telephone rang in the Turnblad kitchen—again.

Edna got up from the couch. "What are we running, a telethon?" she complained.

But she perked up when she heard the voice on the other line.

"Is this the Turnblad residence? Mr. Pinky speaking."

Edna's jaw dropped. It was *the* Mr. Pinky. And then she heard his offer . . .

"*The* Mr. Pinky?" Tracy asked after her mother hung up the phone.

Edna nodded. "From Mr. Pinky's Hefty Hideaway!"

Tracy and Edna shrieked with excitement. They jumped up and down. The living room furniture wobbled and shook. The Hefty Hideaway had gorgeous clothes for all of the plus-sized girls in Baltimore.

"I get to be a spokesgirl! Ooh, tell me I get a free caftan," Tracy said. "Tell me! Tell me!"

"Oh, honey, I think perks like caftans have to be negotiated," Edna said, shaking her head. "Maybe we should get you an agent."

"You be my agent!" Tracy cried.

Edna blushed. "Tracy Turnblad, fame has gone to your head and made you wacky!"

"Why not?" Tracy asked. "Who's going to look out for me better than my mom?"

Edna shook her head. "Me? An agent? You see me hobnobbing and drinking rum and Cokes with those hoi polloi?"

Tracy nodded. "And out-negotiating them!"

"Are you crazy? I haven't left this apartment in years," Edna protested.

"Then it's about time you did," Tracy said. She grabbed her mother's arm and started to pull her toward the door. Edna refused to budge.

"No, no, no, what are you doing?" Edna said, panicking. "I can't be seen!"

"Why not?" Tracy asked.

"After my next diet, we'll go out then," Edna said. "The last time the neighbors saw me, I was a size ten. Please!"

Tracy stopped and looked at her mom. She never realized her mother was embarrassed about how she looked.

"Ma, it's changing out there," Tracy told her. "People who are different . . . their time is coming. Everyone is grooving to a brand-new sound."

Tracy nodded toward the TV. Tracy sang along with the Dynamites. She knew her mom needed to hear these words.

> "Hey mama, hey mama, follow me.
> I know something's in you that you wanna set free.
> So let go, go, go of the past now.
> Say hello to the love in your heart.
> Yes, I know that the world's spinning fast now.
> You got to get yourself a brand-new start."

The Dynamites sang the chorus. "Hey mama. Welcome to the sixties!"

Edna grabbed onto the television, refusing to go. But Tracy didn't give up. She pried Edna's hands off of the TV and led her toward the apartment door.

Edna nervously followed Tracy down the stairs and to the building's front door. She could see people walking up and down the busy street. Cars whizzed by. Edna frowned.

"Welcome to the sixties, Mama!" Tracy said.

Edna gathered her courage. She put one foot out the door. Then another.

"Ma! You did it!" Tracy cried happily.

"I'm a little light-headed," Edna complained. "There's so much air out here. Could we go inside?"

"No, Ma, you're on your way!" Tracy said.

Edna followed Tracy down the streets of Baltimore. Everything around her looked so new and amazing. Girls wearing miniskirts. Giant cars with fancy fins. Kids playing with hula-hoops.

Edna and Tracy walked on. They passed a TV store. On the screen, the Dynamites were still singing their song.

"Welcome to the rhythm of a brand-new day.
Take your old-fashioned fears and just throw

them away!"

Edna found herself dancing along with the music. Soon they arrived in front of Mr. Pinky's Hefty Hideaway. Plus-sized mannequins wearing glamorous dresses stood in the window. A big sign read, "Quality clothes for quantity gals."

When Edna and Tracy walked inside, Mr. Pinky ran up to greet them. He was a short man with a mustache and a loud plaid jacket.

"There's my shining star!" he said, beaming. "Fantastic to meet you. I'm Mr. Pinky. Tracy, is this your older sister?"

Edna blushed. "Oh my!"

"Perhaps she'd like some complimentary couture," Mr. Pinky said. Then he thrust a contract in front of Tracy's face. "Now if you'll just sign here."

Edna waved a finger. "No, no, no. Flattery will not distract Miss Turnblad's agent from reading the fine print!"

Tracy smiled happily. *Go, Mom!* she silently cheered.

"Her agent?" Mr. Pinky asked.

Edna grabbed the contract from him. Her eyes

darted across the pages. Mr. Pinky hovered anxiously beside her.

"Oh no," Edna said, shaking her head. "She's nonexclusive, extension at mutual option. And you absorb my fifteen-percent commission."

"Not a dime over ten," Mr. Pinky replied.

They stared at each other. Then Edna eyed the racks of clothes in the store.

"Throw in a bustier?" she asked.

Mr. Pinky nodded and shook Edna's hand. "Deal!"

Excited, Mr. Pinky led Edna and Tracy into the dressing room area. If Tracy was going to be a spokesgirl for the Hefty Hideaway, she needed to look the part. And, of course, her new agent did, too.

Mr. Pinky snapped his fingers, and three salesgirls appeared. They began to work on Edna, styling her hair and tweezing her eyebrows. Tracy and Mr. Pinky waited outside the dressing room while they fitted Edna in new clothes from top to bottom.

"Step on out!" Mr. Pinky cried.

The salesgirls pulled open the curtain and Edna stepped out, sporting a new, sprayed, Tracy hairdo.

She wore a fabulous pink and gold party dress and high heels. Edna looked in the store mirror. She couldn't believe how beautiful she looked!

The Dynamites' song played on a radio in the Hefty Hideaway. Edna sang along, celebrating her new look.

"Hey Tracy, hey baby, look at me!
I'm the cutest chickie that you ever did see.
Hey Tracy, hey baby, look at us!
Where is there a team that's half as fabulous?"

Then it was Tracy's turn. She went into the dressing room and came out wearing a dress that exactly matched her mom's.

"Welcome to the sixties!" the Dynamites sang. *"Go, mama, go, go, go!"*

Tracy and Edna hugged. They thanked Mr. Pinky and walked back out into the night. To celebrate their new looks, they stopped in a café for a piece of pie.

"Wait till Dad sees you," Tracy said.

Edna sighed. "See me? He doesn't notice what I wear. In twenty years, he's never said 'Nice muumuu' or anything."

"Now he will," Tracy said.

"If he ever leaves his shop for five minutes, maybe," Edna said. She shook her head. "I swear, I don't know what goes on down there."

"Well, Mrs. Turnblad," said a voice nearby. "I'd know whose mother you are anywhere!"

Tracy and Edna looked up to see Velma and Amber standing over them. Velma had a nasty grin on her face.

"Hello, Amber," Tracy said.

"Hello, Tracy," Amber said stiffly.

"Ma, this is Amber Von Tussle and Velma Von Tussle," Tracy said. Edna and Velma shook hands. "Mrs. Von Tussle is the station's manager."

"It's so nice you let her on the show," Edna said.

Velma gave a fake smile. "Tracy certainly has *redefined* our standards," she said.

"That's for sure," Amber agreed. Then they both laughed nastily.

Edna's eyes narrowed.

"Brand-new dress?" Velma asked. "You'll stop traffic."

Velma gave a little wave, and she and Amber left the café. But the damage had been done. Edna turned to Tracy, her lip trembling.

"Ma, don't listen to a word she says," Tracy pleaded.

Edna looked down at her dress. Thanks to Velma, it didn't seem so fabulous anymore.

"I'm taking this back!" she said tearfully.

"Don't you dare!" Tracy said. "Don't you know why she hates us? She's afraid I'll beat Amber for Miss Teenage Hairspray!"

Tracy watched Amber and her mother walk down the street. She didn't care if Amber was mean to her. But being mean to her mom . . . that was another story.

May the best dancer win! Tracy thought.

9

The more popular Tracy became, the nastier Amber grew.

Amber and Tracy were in math class together. That would have been really awful, except Link had the same class, too.

Mr. Flak, their teacher, was writing out some problems on the blackboard. During class, Amber was whispering rumors about Tracy to the girls next to her.

"They can't put Tracy in special ed," Amber said, with fake sympathy. "If I have to tutor her myself, they're not going to hold my friend back."

"You are a saint," one of the girls said.

"And I'm sure it's not true that she has roaches in her hair," Amber whispered. "I'll bet those were just some stray hairs my friend saw, not roach legs."

"Amber, stop it!" Link hissed. "Just because she's a good dancer—"

"You think she can dance?" Amber snapped. "Well, then maybe you'd rather have *her* as your partner. You could get sponsored by the Goodyear blimp!"

Mr. Flak turned from the blackboard. "What's going on back there?" he asked.

Amber pretended she was talking to Tracy.

"Why, Tracy, that's awful. Mr. Flak does *not* have dandruff!" Amber said in a loud whisper.

Mr. Flak brushed some dandruff flakes off of his jacket. Then he glowered at Tracy and pointed at the door. She opened her mouth to protest but knew it wouldn't do any good. She got up and walked to the door.

Link jumped up. He didn't want Tracy to have to leave—it wasn't fair.

"Mr. Larkin. Perhaps you might want to tell us Patrick Henry's immortal last words?" Mr. Flak asked.

"Kiss my butt?" Link tried. The class gasped. When Mr. Flak handed Link a pink detention slip, Link joined Tracy at the door. Tracy flashed Link a grateful smile, and all Amber could do was fume silently in her seat.

When Tracy and Link got to detention, they found

Seaweed, Penny, and the other kids dancing.

"You didn't have to do that, Link," Tracy said.

"Hey—I always wanted to check out the scene down here," Link said.

Tracy's smile faded. She had thought Link was coming to her rescue.

"Right," she said.

Tracy and Link watched as Seaweed tried to teach Penny some moves. "Cool!" Link cried. He jumped in, trying to join the dance. He copied the steps exactly, but he just didn't have any rhythm. Soon the kids in the room were laughing. Tracy laughed, too. She couldn't help it. Link looked so dorky! Still cute—but definitely dorky.

Link grinned and laughed along with them. "Not quite, huh?"

The school bell rang.

"Darn! Just when I was getting it," Link said.

"Well, who says you have to stop?" Seaweed said. "My mom's having a platter party. You all want to come check it out?"

"Now?" Tracy asked. She and Link smiled at each

other. Penny looked a little shocked.

"I've never been to North Avenue before," she said.

"Would it be safe?" Link asked. "You know—for us?"

"It's cool, white boy," Seaweed answered.

Penny turned to Tracy. "Wow! Being invited places by black people!"

"It feels so hip!" Tracy agreed.

"Glad you feel that way, friends, 'cause not everybody does," Seaweed said. "Sometimes when people look at me, all they see is the color of my face. I'm proud of who I am, and I'm tired of having to hide it. Maybe if you all come and see where I'm from you'll understand a little better."

"Sure," Tracy said as she, Link, and Penny walked down the hall with the detention kids.

A girl ran up to Seaweed and hugged him. Tracy recognized her as the girl that Velma threw out of the Corny Collins audition.

"Tracy, this is my sister, Little Inez," Seaweed said.

"Oh, I know Tracy Turnblad," Little Inez said. "Good for you, girl! You got on the show."

"Well, you better be next!" Tracy said.

Tracy Turnblad before . . .

And after . . .

Amber Von Tussle— the not-so-"Nicest Kid in Town"

Penny and Tracy watching The Corny Collins Show

Tracy dreams of dancing in front of the whole world!

Tracy twistin' in detention with Seaweed and his friends

Tracy shows off the "Peyton Place After Midnight" dance at the hop

Penny Pingleton— Tracy's best friend

Tracy's debut on The Corny Collins Show

Tracy welcomes her mother to the '60s with a hip new look!

Motormouth Maybelle is "Big, Blonde, and Beautiful!"

Tracy takes a stand!

Amber competes in the Miss Teenage Hairspray Pageant

Link and Tracy prove that "You Can't Stop the Beat!"

It was love at first sight for Link and Tracy!

Little Inez nodded. "You got that right! I'm tired of covering up all my pride. I know I can dance as good as any of those council girls—I just need someone to give me a chance."

Tracy nodded. She knew how Little Inez felt.

Tracy and the others walked toward the bus lines. The white kids got in line for one bus. The black kids got in line for another bus. Tracy, Penny, and Link got in line with the black kids.

Amber watched Link climb on the bus in horror. Link was her boyfriend! What was he doing with Tracy Turnblad and those detention losers?

"Link! Link!" she yelled as she ran to the bus. "Where do you think you're going?"

The bus doors closed in Amber's face.

"Link!" Amber cried as she helplessly watched the bus pull away.

Amber stomped her foot.

"Motherrrrrrrrrrr!" she screamed.

Nobody on the bus heard Amber's tantrum. They were too busy listening to the radio, dancing, and having

fun. Seaweed did a backflip and ended up in the seat next to Penny. They smiled adoringly at each other.

Soon the bus pulled to a stop on North Avenue. The kids climbed out and ran down the street. Seaweed led them through the doors of a huge record shop.

Motormouth Maybelle was singing along to a record on the record player. No one could stop themselves from dancing to the song.

"Bring on that pecan pie!
Pour some sugar on it, honey, don't be shy.
Scoop me up a mess of that chocolate swirl.
Don't be stingy—I'm a growing girl!
I offer big love with no apology.
How can I deny the world the most of me?
I'm not afraid to throw my weight around.
Pound by pound by pound.
Because I'm big, blond, and beautiful!
Face the fact—it's simply irrefutable!
No one wants a meal that only offers the least,
When, girl, we're serving up the whole darn feast!"

Maybelle stopped singing when she noticed the white kids in her shop.

"Well! Looks like you all took a step out of bounds," she said. "Now who've we got here?"

Seaweed introduced his friends. "This is my mom, Motormouth Maybelle. Mom, this is Link, Tracy—"

"This is so Afro-tastic!" Tracy chimed in.

"And Penny Pingleton," Seaweed said, smiling.

"I'm very pleased and scared to be here," Penny said.

Maybelle took Penny's hands in hers. "Honey, we got more reason to be scared on *your* street," she said.

Once all the introductions were made, everybody got back to dancing.

Tracy got into the groove right away. Link had a little more trouble—but he tried.

Seaweed waved Penny over to him and took her hands in his. When they danced together there was an electricity between them—everyone could see it.

Things were definitely not grooving at the Von Tussle house. Amber sprawled on her bed and buried her face in her pillow, sobbing.

"He danced right onto that bus with the Great White Whale and a bunch of Negroes," Amber sobbed.

"Honey, reeling him back in is the easiest thing in the world," Velma said. "Remember, I control his career."

"But why is Tracy so popular?" Amber wailed. "We'll never get her off the show!"

"You're right. We won't," Velma said. She broke into a grin. "Her mother will *pull* her off the show."

Amber raised her head and listened to her mother's devious plan.

Amber wiped the tears from her face. She got up and grabbed a scarf from her dresser. Then she picked up her pink telephone and had the operator connect her to the Turnblads' apartment.

Edna answered on the other line.

"Never mind who this is," Amber said, holding the scarf over her mouth to disguise her voice. "I have information about your daughter's whereabouts. Right as we speak she has entered a hotbed of moral turpentine!"

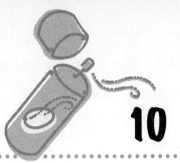

10

Back in Maybelle's shop, the kids danced until the sun went down. When a slow song played on the radio, Penny rested her head on Seaweed's shoulder and they began to dance. Tracy and Link gazed into each other's eyes.

"Link, aren't you going to get in awful trouble for this?" Tracy asked.

"I'm not planning on telling my Dad," Link answered.

"No, I mean . . . with someone else," Tracy said. As much as she didn't like Amber, she didn't want to steal anyone's boyfriend.

Link's blue eyes smiled down at Tracy. "Maybe I will. But maybe it's worth it," he answered. "I think knowing you is the start of a pretty big adventure."

Tracy's heart began to beat faster. She could hear those bells chiming inside her head again.

"TRACY EDNA TURNBLAD!"

Edna stood in the doorway, furious. Maybelle stopped the music.

"We get any more white people in here it'll be a suburb," she joked.

"Do you know what I had to pay a cab to even consider coming down here?" Edna yelled. She marched toward Tracy. "No call! You just disappear? So I finally find my 'responsible' daughter twisting the night away in the ghetto?"

"Um, Edna Turnblad, this is Link," Tracy said nervously.

Edna grabbed Tracy's arm. "And all mashed up against a crooner? Come on. We're going. Penny, go home before your mother shoots you."

Penny let go of Seaweed, blinking in fear.

"Oh now, Miss Edna, you don't have to rush off," Maybelle said, walking up to Edna.

"Yes I do! I left the iron on," Edna replied.

Maybelle pointed toward the back room of the shop. Maybelle and the kids lived in the apartment there. The dining room table was set for dinner. It was covered with plates piled with fried chicken, ribs, corn

68

bread, coleslaw, and all kinds of delicious soul food.

"Before you go, you sure you won't have a little something to eat?" Maybelle asked.

Edna was tempted. She pointed to a pot of brisket on the table. "Is that braised?"

Maybelle grinned and sang some more of her song.

"We're big, blond, and beautiful.

There is nothing 'bout us that's unsuitable.

Why sit in the bleachers timid and afraid?

When Edna, you can be the whole parade!"

That was all Edna needed to hear. She sat down at the table and joined the feast. Maybelle turned the music back on, and the kids continued dancing.

"Miss Maybelle, you do throw a very lively party," Edna said, after downing a plate of brisket. "What are you celebrating?"

"Well, it's kind of an ending," Maybelle said, a little sadly. "It deserved to go out with a bang."

"What ended?" Penny asked.

"Negro Day," Maybelle replied.

Everyone stopped dancing. They looked at Maybelle, shocked.

"All right," Maybelle said. "Time you all knew. Velma Von Tussle just told me that we've had our last show. Said the show was a nice little placeholder, but it was time to get some ratings. I didn't want to tell you all up front . . . I wanted a little joy tonight."

"But I practiced so hard!" Little Inez cried.

Maybelle put a hand on her daughter's shoulder. "And you will be seen, baby. I promise you that."

Tracy's mind was racing. Life had been amazing since she got on *The Corny Collins Show*. But some things were more important than being famous. More important than dancing, even.

"You can't have your own show? Fine! You'll come dance with us!" Tracy announced.

Maybelle raised a blond eyebrow. "Honey, you been dozing off during history?"

"Yes, always!" Tracy replied.

"Ain't no blacks and whites ever danced together on TV," Seaweed said. "There's a whole lotta Velmas out there."

Tracy knew Seaweed was right. But there had to be some way . . .

"Well, if we can't dance, maybe we should just march," Tracy said finally.

Maybelle nodded. "That'd get some big old ratings."

Tracy grinned. "Bigger time slot, too."

"Like on the eleven o'clock news!" Maybelle shouted.

Everyone in the shop shouted and cheered.

"Wha'cha all say?" Maybelle asked. "Should we give this fine woman the ratings she deserves?"

"Yeah!" everyone cried. Well, almost everyone.

"Well, it's a school night," Edna said, standing up from the table. "I really think we should call it a—"

"We meet at the church, Friday," Maybelle called out. "We march on WYZT! It's time!"

"Yeah!" Tracy shouted along with the others.

Edna walked up to Tracy, shaking her head. "Oh no, now, no—don't mistake me—these are fine, fine people—but you can't protest with them!"

Tracy ignored her mom. She walked over to Link, her eyes shining.

"Link! We're going with them, right?" she asked.

"Trace," Link began in a soft voice. "I've been smiling

and dancing on this show for three years. Mrs. Von Tussle just promised I can sing at the Miss Teenage Hairspray pageant. She's invited agents . . . that's my shot, Trace. I just can't jeopardize that."

Tracy couldn't believe it. "But . . . it's what's right," she said.

Link looked into Tracy's eyes. She could tell that this decision was hard for him.

"I'm sorry, Trace. I think maybe this adventure's . . . a little too big for me," he said quietly.

Too *big*? Tracy was stunned. She thought Link was different . . . that he liked her for who she was and that her weight didn't matter.

"Oh no!" Link said quickly. "You know I didn't mean—"

Link hadn't meant to hurt Tracy, but she was too upset to see that. She tried with all her might to hold back tears.

"I get it, Link. It's your shot," she said, walking toward her mother.

Link wanted to run to Tracy, but he felt torn up inside. He liked her—he really did. But he didn't want

to jeopardize his big chance.

Link felt helpless. He knew nothing he could say would make Tracy understand.

"I should go," he said softly.

As Link left the shop, Edna gave Tracy a hug.

"Give him time," she said. "He'll figure out he's crazy about you."

"You have to say that," Tracy said glumly. "You're my mother."

"Well, I know a little something about men," Edna assured her.

Maybelle walked up and put her arm around Edna and Tracy.

"You look like you could use something to eat," she offered.

After another plate of brisket, Tracy and Edna headed home. When they walked past the Hardy Har Hut, they saw a light on inside.

"He's always in there, working late," Edna said, as they walked up the stairs. "Do I take it personal? Nah. They always put their career first."

"I'm going to grab a snack and go to bed," Tracy

said. She gave her mom a kiss. "I love you."

"Love you, too, babe," Edna replied, heading for her bedroom. It had been a long day, but she was excited for Wilbur to see her glamorous makeover. She just needed to freshen up a little, and then she'd surprise Wilbur at the store.

Meanwhile, in her own bedroom, Tracy wasn't feeling excited at all. She knew marching on Friday could get her into a lot of trouble. She'd rather be dancing on the show with Link, but how could she dance when Seaweed and other black people couldn't? Unless everyone could dance, dancing was no fun at all. Why couldn't Link see that?

Tracy sighed and stared out the window. Today, she had almost become Link Larkin's girlfriend.

And now she'd lost him forever.

11

Now it was time for Velma to put her part of the plan into motion.

After Amber called Edna Turnblad, Velma put on a slinky red dress. She knew it wouldn't be long before Edna would be back from North Avenue.

Velma made her way downtown to the Hardy Har Hut. The bell on the door jingled as she stepped inside. Boxes of all kinds of things filled the store's crowded shelves: trick gum, whoopee cushions, and plastic flowers that squirted water. Velma stared around the shop, wondering where Wilbur might be.

"Hello?" she called out.

A gorilla mask answered her. "Hiya!"

Velma screamed in shock.

"Welcome to the Hardy Har Hut!" said Wilbur as he pulled the gorilla mask off his head. "So what can I do you for? Something for the mister?"

75

"Sadly, there is no mister at the moment," Velma answered.

"A beautiful woman like yourself?" Wilbur asked.

Velma batted her long eyelashes, trying to look sweet and innocent. "My husband accidentally suffocated."

Wilbur thought for a moment, then snapped his fingers.

"So, you need a fella," he said.

"Yes," Velma said, stepping closer to Wilbur. "I need a fella."

Wilbur nodded. "The way to a man's heart is through his funny bone. Now here's an icebreaker for ya!"

He grabbed a plastic ice cube from the shelf and held it up to her face. A fly was trapped inside.

"Slip this into the seltzer of some Johnnie at your next soiree," he said, wiggling his eyebrows.

Velma gave Wilbur a fake smile. Inside she was seething.

Her plan had been simple. Charm Wilbur Turnblad and make Edna Turnblad jealous. If her plan went right, Edna would pull Tracy off of the TV show.

But Wilbur didn't seem to notice that Velma was

coming on to him—not even one tiny bit. He rushed around the shop, pulling out gags for her to try.

"We got your clown nose, your Groucho nose, your elephant nose. You want Belgian chocolate animal droppings? This store's for you!" Wilbur said proudly.

"What a treasure trove," Velma said, trying to sound interested.

Wilbur pulled out a pair of glasses with swirls on the lenses. He grinned.

"And my personal favorite! X-ray specs!" he said. "You can use them to see through anything."

Velma walked up to Wilbur. She took off his glasses.

"You don't need special glasses to see the truth, Wilbur," she said in a sultry voice. "And the truth is I think you're a very handsome man."

Wilbur was very confused. "I'm not sure what you mean."

"Kiss me, Wilbur," said Velma as she grabbed Wilbur by his suspenders.

At that very moment, Edna walked into the Hardy Har Hut.

"You!" Edna cried in horror.

"You?" Velma responded, with fake surprise.

"Hi, Edna!" Wilbur said cheerfully. He really had no idea how bad things looked.

But Edna had seen all she needed to see. She ran out of the shop and slammed the door behind her.

Velma's plan worked. The next day, *The Corny Collins Show* went on the air—without Tracy.

"I'm Amber!"

"Brad!"

"Tammy!"

"I.Q.!"

"Lou Ann!"

"I'm . . . Amber!"

At the break, Corny walked up to Velma, annoyed.

"Your daughter can't say her name twice!" he said.

"Oh? Does it say that on a stone tablet?" Velma asked. "Besides, we haven't filled Turnblad's spot yet."

"It's not like Tracy not to show," Corny said. "What happened to her, Velma?"

"How in the world would I know?" Velma answered innocently. She flounced off.

Corny eyed Velma suspiciously as she walked away. He knew something strange was going on.

Meanwhile, back in the Turnblad apartment, Edna sobbed at the kitchen table. Tracy sat next to her, miserable.

"Ma, you don't really believe—" Tracy began.

"You are never setting foot on that show again!" Edna said firmly. "Do you hear me?"

Tracy sighed. "I heard you the first four hundred times, Ma."

Tracy felt bad for her mom, but she knew her dad would never do anything to hurt her mom. To find out what really happened, she'd have to go to the Hardy Har Hut.

When Tracy got to the shop, all the lights in the shop were off except for a small night-light. In the darkness, Tracy could make out the shape of her dad sleeping on the floor.

Tracy sat down on a chair next to her father. "Dad—"

"Tracy, you know these peepers have never looked at another woman!" Wilbur said. "This heart only

beats for a size sixty!"

He rolled back over, trying to get comfortable.

"Daddy, you know what Velma wanted," Tracy said. "She wanted me off the show. And I knew that, but how she could go that far—try to hurt you and Ma—" She started to cry.

"Come here, little girl," Wilbur said gently.

Tracy knelt down and hugged her dad.

"And then Velma canceled Negro Day," Tracy told him. "Just to make sure that nobody who's different— who's black or Chinese, or . . . maybe who needs to lose a few pounds . . ."

Wilbur smiled weakly. He understood.

"And you know, I think I've kind of been in a bubble or something," Tracy went on. "Thinking that fairness was gonna just . . . happen. It's not. I think people like me are going to have to get up off their father's laps and go and fight for it."

"Tracy, your mother and I . . . we don't get too far past our front door. But you see all the way to Schenectady," Wilbur said, smiling at his daughter. "So if there's something you need to stand up for, don't you listen to old dogs like us. We need to learn some new tricks from you."

"You don't need new tricks, Dad," Tracy said. "You need Mom."

Wilbur's smile faded. "She changed the locks," he said gloomily.

Tracy grinned and held up a shiny silver key.

Upstairs, Edna was sitting at the kitchen table, reading a book. Wilbur tiptoed up next to her. Edna put the book right in front of her face.

"Think about me, honey," Wilbur said. "Took me five years to figure out you were flirting. How could I ever—"

Edna slowly lowered the book.

"Well. She is very . . . glamorous," Edna said. "She makes me feel old."

"Nonsense, doll," Wilbur said. "You're as spry as a Slinky!"

Edna got up and went over to the laundry pile. She started sorting clothes. She wasn't quite ready to face Wilbur yet.

Wilbur didn't give up. "Edna, the world is changing

every day," he said. "But you're timeless to me."

Edna pretended like he wasn't there and tried to walk past him.

"You're like a stinky old cheese, just getting better with age!" Wilbur said as Edna pushed past him.

Wilbur blocked her path. "You're like a fatal disease, and I don't want the cure!" he said. Edna walked right past him. She went outside and started taking clothes off of the laundry line.

Wilbur stopped her and took her hands in his.

"Every day with you is like a gift, Edna," he said softly. "You're first-rate, babe. And face it—you're stuck with me till the bitter end."

A slow smile appeared on Edna's face. Wilbur led her around the tiny garden, dancing.

"Oh, Wilbur," Edna said. "You're timeless to me, too!"

From her window, Tracy watched her dancing parents and grinned.

Turnblads 1, Velma 0.

She climbed back into bed.

Tomorrow was Friday. And without a doubt, Tracy knew exactly what she needed to do.

12

The next morning, Edna burst into Tracy's room, beaming with happiness.

"Good morning, sweetie!" she said happily. "Everything's all better."

Tracy didn't move. Suspicious, Edna pulled the covers off of the bed.

She gasped. A stuffed armchair was there in Tracy's place!

Across town, Tracy walked toward the church on North Avenue. She knew her mom was nervous about her going to the march, but she also knew she had to go.

A huge crowd of people—mostly black—gathered in front of the church. Tracy found Maybelle, Seaweed, and some of the kids from detention at the head of the crowd. She grabbed a sign that read INTEGRATION NOW! and joined them.

Maybelle nodded at Tracy. "You're gonna pay a price," she warned her.

"I know," Tracy said.

"You'll never dance on TV again," Maybelle said.

"If I can't dance with Seaweed and Little Inez, then I won't dance at all," Tracy said, and she meant it.

Maybelle put her hand on Tracy's shoulder and began to sing. Her voice rang out from the steps of the church.

> *"There's a light in the darkness,*
> *Though the light is as black as my skin.*
> *There's a light burning bright, showing me*
> *the way . . .*
> *But I know where I've been."*

Maybelle walked down the church steps. The crowd followed her as she marched down the street. Maybelle kept singing.

> *"There's a road we've been travelin',*
> *Lost so many on the way.*
> *But the riches will be plenty,*
> *Worth the price, the price we had to pay."*

The crowd marched down the streets of Baltimore

toward the TV station. One by one, more people joined the march. Gas station attendants, delivery boys, businessmen, secretaries . . . all kinds of people.

Maybelle's voice swelled over the crowd.

> *"There's a dream in the future.*
> *There's a struggle we have yet to win.*
> *Use that pride in our hearts to lift us to tomorrow,*
> *'Cause just to sit still would be a sin.*
> *Lord knows I know where I've been.*
> *I'll give thanks to my God*
> *'Cause I know where I've been!"*

Tracy felt more confident with each step she took. She might have lost everything—stardom, Link—but she knew in her heart that she was doing the right thing, the only thing she could do and stay true to herself.

As they neared the TV station, Edna came running up, breathless.

"Tracy, honey! You don't know what you're doing," Edna said. She nodded to Maybelle. "Evening, Ms. Maybelle."

"Yes I do, Ma!" Tracy protested.

"Good evening, Mrs. Edna," Maybelle said. "How nice of you to join us."

Tracy kept walking. Edna followed, pulling at Tracy's sleeve.

"Honey, she's got a lovely turnout," Edna said anxiously. "She really doesn't need you along."

Tracy linked arms with her mother and they both got swept up in the crowd of marchers. Edna looked around for some way to get out, but the crowd filled every inch of the street.

When the marchers turned the corner, they found huge police barricades blocking the way to the WYZT television station. Police officers waited, their guns drawn. News reporters stood by, their cameras and notepads poised. Only the WYZT news cameras were missing from the scene.

The protesters began to shout and wave their signs.

"Two, four, six, eight! TV's got to integrate!" Tracy shouted along as loud as she could.

As they got closer to the barricade, Edna started to panic.

"Oh my gosh. No, no!" she wailed.

"Ma, come on! You knew there'd be police here," Tracy said.

"Police, yes. I didn't know there'd be cameras!" Edna cried. "I cannot be seen on television at my present weight!"

From the window of her office, Velma watched the scene with an evil grin. She had a few connections at the police station. She would be calling in a few favors today.

Down below, the protesters kept their cool. They didn't want to cause any trouble. They just wanted to get their message out. Maybelle walked up to the police sergeant, a pleasant smile on her face.

"Excuse me, is there some reason we can't pass by peacefully here?" she asked.

The officer shot Maybelle a dirty look. "Ma'am, I strongly suggest you and your little friends head back to where you came from."

Then he turned his back on her. Tracy couldn't believe how he was treating Maybelle.

"Hey! You don't have to be so rude," Tracy said.

The officer didn't even bother to turn around to respond.

"Tracy!" Edna warned.

"I can handle this, Tracy," Maybelle chimed in.

But Tracy was angry. Police officers were supposed to help people, not ignore them. She tapped the sergeant on the shoulder.

"Excuse me," she said politely.

The sergeant turned around, his eyes dark and angry.

"You just assaulted a police officer, miss!" he said.

"Assaulted?" Tracy didn't know what to say to such a ridiculous charge.

"My daughter would never do that!" Edna protested.

Other people in the crowd spoke up in Tracy's defense. This only seemed to make the sergeant angrier.

"Enough! Enough!" he yelled. "Boys, let's arrest the whole lot!"

The police officers held up billy clubs and handcuffs.

"Uh-oh," Seaweed said. "Time to go!"

The protesters instantly panicked and ran off in

different directions. As Seaweed grabbed Tracy's hand and led her through the chaos, Edna stood her ground. She was blocking the path so the police couldn't get to Tracy.

Then Edna felt a strong arm on her shoulder.

"Ma'am, you're under arrest!"

13

Tracy and Seaweed got away, but many of the protesters were arrested.

Edna lined up behind Maybelle and some of the other women protesters as they were handcuffed and herded into a police wagon. Edna noticed that she was the only white person in line—and the only person who hadn't been handcuffed. A police officer spotted her in the line.

"You can go," he said.

"I can?" Edna asked, confused.

"Yeah, go on, ma'am," the officer said.

"Edna, honey, do what he says," Maybelle told her.

"But why do I get to go home?" Edna asked. "I did the same as you."

"And we won't be forgetting it soon," Maybelle said softly.

"Shut up," the officer said rudely to Maybelle. He

turned to Edna. "Move along, ma'am."

He started to push some of the protesters into the wagon. Edna didn't move.

"Why are you calling me ma'am and telling them to shut up?" she asked, angrily. "I think you owe them an apology."

"What?" the officer asked. Was this woman for real?

"I believe you heard me," Edna said, hands on her hips.

"Oooh! Sister Edna's in it now!" Maybelle said.

"Last chance," the officer said to Edna. "Shut your trap and go home."

Edna faced the officer and looked him in the eyes. "No. Last chance for you," she said, her voice rising. "You apologize to these people, who have done nothing illegal. And you let them go home to their families this minute!"

The police officer paused for a moment. Then he made a decision. He snapped the handcuffs on Edna's wrists.

"Ed-na! Ed-na!" the women on line began to chant.

Edna climbed into the police wagon with the other protesters. They were all taken to the station house,

processed, and locked in jail.

A few hours later, Edna was relieved to hear a police officer call her name. When he let her out of the cell, Wilbur was waiting for her. The two drove home and immediately checked to see if Tracy was in the apartment.

"Tracy?" she called out.

"She's not here, hon," Wilbur said. "She knows if the cops are looking for her, this is the first place they'd come."

Edna shook her head. "Wilbur, what this must've put you through . . . I'm so sorry!"

"I'm not," Wilbur said. "I'm proud of you, baby. Somebody had to do something. Course we may be eating beans for a few years . . . bail for twenty people's kinda pricey."

A look of shock came over Edna's face. "Wilbur, you bailed out all those people?"

"Oh, honey, ya upset with me?" Wilbur said nervously. "I'm sorry. It just seemed like the right thing—"

Edna flung herself into Wilbur's arms. "Oh, Wilbur,

knights in armor don't come any shinier than you," she said, squeezing him tightly. "Oh, where's our little girl?"

In the Pingleton house, Penny sat on the couch with her mother, watching the news. There was Tracy, right on the screen—running away from the police!

"And our cameras also caught Tracy Turnblad, the teenaged TV personality and rabble-rouser," the anchorman was saying. "Miss Turnblad brutally attacked a sergeant with a blunt instrument before fleeing the scene."

Then Penny saw something out of the corner of her eye. It was Tracy—in person! Her face was pressed against the living room window.

Penny's face went white and she nodded toward her mother. Tracy understood. She nodded back, and Penny quickly turned back to the TV.

"There is a warrant out for Tracy Turnblad's arrest," the news anchor was saying.

"You see? You see?" Prudy Pingleton squeaked. "If I ever let you leave this house, right now you'd be in

prison! That Tracy Turnblad always was a bad influence. You will never see that depraved girl again!"

Upstairs, Tracy climbed in through Penny's bedroom window. She waited and waited. Then Penny opened the door.

"Mom's asleep," Penny whispered. "Follow me. I know where you can hide."

Penny led Tracy downstairs to the basement. They tiptoed across the concrete floor.

"Thanks, Pen," Tracy said in a low voice. "You're a great friend. The cops are looking for me everywhere. You could go to jail for helping me."

"Tracy, I'm already in jail," Penny sighed.

She opened the door to a small cement room. The girls walked inside. Penny flicked a light switch. A single lightbulb flickered on overhead.

"Oh noooo!" Penny wailed.

"Someone's coming?" Tracy asked.

"No, your hair's deflating!" Penny pointed out.

Tracy reached up and patted her hair. Penny was right. A day of being on the run had left her hair flat as a pancake. Normally, that would have made Tracy cry.

"Let it deflate," Tracy said coolly. "It was just a symbol of my conformity to the Man."

"Ooh, you are so tough!" Penny said admiringly. She gestured around at the tiny room. "So what do you think? Maybe you could live here. There's food, water, and a first-aid kit."

"It's very well insulated," Tracy said, impressed. She walked over to a shelf filled with cans of food. Being on the run had also made her very hungry.

"You won't be needing that!" a cold voice snapped.

The girls turned and saw Penny's mom standing in the doorway.

"The police are on their way," Prudy informed them.

"Oh, Mother, please don't send my best friend to the big house!" Penny begged.

Prudy pulled Penny through the door.

"You haven't heard the last of me, Mrs. Pingleton," Tracy promised. "I won't stop trying to change things. I don't care how long it takes!"

"Good. 'Cause you'll be waiting twenty years to

life!" Prudy said. Then she slammed the door shut and locked the door from the outside.

Tracy leaned her head against the cement wall. This was it. The end of the line.

A new song filled her heart. It wasn't a love song or a happy song. It was a song of hope and determination.

> "If I can just stay true to the steps I've taken,
> It will all come through.
> I'll let fate set the date.
> It's okay, I can wait.
> Plant the tiniest seed down below,
> Tend it well then stand back and just watch it grow.
> Watch me grow.
> If I can just stay true to the steps I've taken,
> It will all come through.
> Name the date and say when,
> But till then,
> I can wait."

Edna and Wilbur watched the news in their living

room, hoping for a sign from Tracy. But the story got exaggerated more and more with each retelling.

"A massive manhunt is underway for Tracy Turnblad, who bludgeoned decorated Korean War veteran Sergeant Mike Morris with a crowbar, shattering his jaw," the anchor announced. "Sergeant Morris is in critical condition."

A picture flashed on the screen of the sergeant in a scout leader uniform, talking to a group of adorable Boy Scouts.

Edna fanned her face with her hand. She was so nervous that she couldn't stop perspiring. She walked over to the window and opened it. The sound of police sirens filled the night. Flashing lights lit up the living room.

"Oh, this is such a Midol moment!" Edna moaned.

Now another police officer was being interviewed. "Uh, we've had a little trouble pinpointing her location," he was saying. "We've gotten thirty-three different tips on Miss Turnblad's whereabouts."

As the interview continued, Wilbur was on the phone. "Hello?" he said, in a voice that sounded like

an old lady's. "Yes, I think I've seen that Turnblond creature! I'm at 101 South Park Road. Thank you, dear." He'd do anything to protect his daughter.

A frantic knock on the door added to the noise and confusion. Edna opened it to find Link Larkin standing there, his blue eyes filled with concern.

"Good evening, Mrs. Turnblad," Link said politely. "I'm so sorry to bother you, but I was at home practicing my new twist on the Twist and I overheard it on the news. All three channels."

"I know," Edna said.

"I can't believe that Tracy savagely bludgeoned an Eagle Scout," Link said. "It's just not like her."

"No, it isn't, hon," Edna said gently.

Link took a deep breath. "I should have been there. Beside her."

Edna wrapped him in a big bear hug.

"Why don't you come in, dear," she told him.

14

Back at Penny's house, Tracy pulled and pulled on the basement door, but it was no use.

Upstairs in Penny's bedroom, Mrs. Pingleton was tying Penny's arms behind her back.

"Penny Lou Pingleton, you are absolutely, positively, permanently punished!" Prudy said, her head bobbing up and down like a chicken's. "You will live on a diet of saltines and Tang, and you will never leave this room again!"

Prudy left the room, slamming the door behind her. Penny sighed. Her mom could get really paranoid sometimes.

Then Penny heard a noise at the window. She craned her neck to see Seaweed climbing in.

"Shhh! Don't let her hear you!" Penny warned.

"What happened?" Seaweed asked.

"She's punishing me for harboring a fugitive without

her permission," Penny said. "What are you doing?"

Seaweed started to untie Penny's knots.

"Rescuing the fair maiden," he said as he gazed into Penny's eyes.

Penny gazed right back at him. They leaned toward each other and kissed.

"Oh, you *do* care!" Penny cried. "I was afraid the colors of our skin would keep us apart."

"No!" Seaweed said, shaking his head. He quickly worked to undo the knots. "Wow, these knots are something else. Was your mama in the navy?"

Back at the Turnblads' apartment, Link wandered through Tracy's small bedroom. He felt closer to her, being here. He lovingly touched Tracy's can of hairspray. Then he picked up her framed high school picture that sat on her dresser.

Link had been wrong . . . so wrong. He should have marched at Tracy's side. They should be together, but now Tracy was all alone out there. As he gazed at the photo, a single tear slid down his cheek. He wished that Tracy were right in front of him. A song rose up

from the depths of his heart.

>"*Once I was a selfish fool who never understood.*
>
>*I never looked inside myself, though on the outside I looked good!*
>
>*Then we met and you made me the man I am today.*
>
>*Tracy, I'm in love with you no matter what you weigh!*"

Over at Penny's house, Seaweed untied the last knot. Penny jumped up and hugged him. She was in love for the first time ever—and it was the best feeling in the world.

Seaweed thought so, too. He sang as the climbed down the trellis on the side of Penny's house.

"*Without love, life is like a beat that you can't follow,*" Seaweed sang.

"*Without love, life is Doris Day at the Apollo!*" Penny chimed in.

Then their voices joined together in perfect harmony.

"Darling, I'll be yours forever, 'cause I never wanna be

Without love.

So darling never set me free!"

They ran to the street where Seaweed's friends were waiting for them in Stooey's car. Penny was about to climb in when she remembered something—TRACY!

She ran to the basement window and placed a set of keys in Tracy's outstretched hand.

Tracy let herself out of the basement and hopped into the trunk of Stooey's car. Moments later, the car raced around the corner. As they neared North Avenue, they saw a roadblock up ahead. Stooey slowed to a stop.

A police officer with a flashlight walked over to the car and shone the light inside. He saw one skinny white girl, but no Tracy Turnblad. With a nod, he waved the car on.

Inside the trunk of the car, Tracy breathed a sigh of relief. Through the metal, she heard Penny and Seaweed crooning their love for each other. Tracy longed to see Link again, at least one more time. She knew somehow, in her heart, that he truly loved her, too.

It wasn't long before the car pulled up in front of Maybelle's record shop. When Stooey opened the trunk, Tracy climbed out and joined in the song.

"Like a week that's only Mondays.

Only ice cream, never sundaes.

Like a circle with no center.

Like a door marked 'do not enter.'

Darling, I'll be yours forever

'Cause I never wanna be

Without love!"

Maybelle and Little Inez walked in through the back of the store, wearing their nightgowns. They looked surprised to see the singing and dancing kids.

Seaweed noticed his mom staring at them. He stopped dancing. He wasn't sure how Maybelle would feel about harboring a fugitive—or a white girlfriend, for that matter.

"Mama . . . I . . ." His voice trailed off.

"You want to hide her here?" Maybelle asked with a raised eyebrow.

Seaweed looked down at his shoes. Maybelle broke into a big grin and playfully whacked him on the head.

"Well, why didn't you think of that before?" she asked. "After what she did for us? Where are your manners, boy?"

Seaweed grinned back at his mom, relieved. Maybelle turned to go back to bed, then stopped. She looked at Penny.

"And what about this one?" she asked.

"Seaweed's got a girlfriend!" Little Inez teased.

Maybelle looked Penny over. "Oh. So this is love," she said finally.

Seaweed and Penny nodded, a little embarrassed.

"Well, love is a gift," Maybelle told them. "But not everyone remembers that. So you two better brace yourselves for a whole lot of ugly comin' at you from a never-ending parade of stupid."

"Oh, so you know my mom," Penny said.

Tracy suddenly felt completely exhausted—but she couldn't rest now. She couldn't go on being a fugitive the rest of her life. And she certainly couldn't let Velma Von Tussle win.

One good thing had come out of being locked in the Pingletons' basement. Tracy had time to think—

and to plan.

She called her mom from Maybelle's phone.

"Mom—yes, I'm safe!" she said. "Now listen. I need your help. You know what day tomorrow is?"

After Tracy explained the plan to her mom, she put down the receiver and smiled.

Tomorrow, whether Velma liked it or not, things were going to change at WYZT.

15

The next morning, people from all over Baltimore headed to the WYZT TV station. It was time to crown Miss Teenage Hairspray 1962!

The pageant was always a big event. Corny's dance council dressed in formal clothes. The boys wore white tuxedo jackets with black pants, and the girls wore their frilliest party dresses. The council entertained the audience by singing songs and leading dances. Throughout the show, viewers could call in their votes for Miss Teenage Hairspray.

A long line snaked around the building as hopeful fans waited to be part of the studio audience. A giant can of Ultra-Clutch Hairspray stood by the door. Mr. Spritzer wanted to make sure everyone remembered to buy his hairspray.

Police officers checked everyone in line, looking for Tracy. Luckily, they weren't looking for Edna. She entered the station wearing an overcoat and a scarf over her head. She stood on the sidelines, sizing up the studio. Star-shaped lights dangled over the stage. A scoreboard read MISS TEENAGE HAIRSPRAY 1962. Amber was leading Tracy by just a few votes.

Finally, the lights dimmed and Corny stepped onstage wearing a shiny silver jacket. Some of the dance council stood behind him.

"And now, broadcast in front of a live studio audience for the first time, from our certified, up-to-code WYZT studio, it's the event of a lifetime!" Corny announced, grinning. "The crescendo of a young girl's dream—it's the Corny Collins Miss Teenage Hairspray Spectacular!"

"*He's Corny!*" sang the council members.

"Brought to you by Ultra-Clutch Hairspray!" Corny said. Then he launched into the Ultra-Clutch theme song.

> "*What gives a girl power and punch?*
> *Is it charm? Is it poise?*
> *No, it's hairspray!*"

While Corny entertained onstage, Velma was up to

no good backstage. She collected the tally cards from the phone operators. Most of the cards had votes for Tracy on them.

Velma slyly replaced the cards with ones with Amber's name on them. She handed them to the scoreboard operator with a smile. Then she took a walkie-talkie from her purse and pressed a button.

"Well?" she asked.

The chief of police had the other walkie-talkie. He stood outside the TV station with several police officers. They held back a crowd of people who desperately wanted to get into the studio.

"No sign of her," he responded into the walkie-talkie. "We're on every door. She's not inside."

"That doesn't mean she won't try!" Velma hissed.

"Velma, I seriously doubt this girl is going to risk incarceration to win a pageant!" the chief answered.

"Well, I know *I* would!" Velma said. "Do you have the warrant with you?"

The chief nodded. "Yup. And handcuffs. Extra large."

"Good. Just keep looking!" Velma snapped.

As Corny Collins was finishing his song, Amber and

Link stood backstage. They were waiting to go on.

"Link, the Hollywood agents are here!" Amber cried as she peered into the crowd. "Look!"

Link saw an usher show two men in jazzy-looking suits and sunglasses to the front row.

"Maybe they'll sign us together!" Amber said happily.

Link gave a low groan. The agents were the whole reason he hadn't marched with Tracy. But without Tracy at his side, being famous would be no fun at all.

The crowd clapped as Corny sang his last note.

"And we're out!" said the stage manager. Link and Amber ran onstage to take their places during the commercial break.

The stage lights flared back on and Corny grinned.

"And now for the talent portion of our competition!" he said. "Our councilettes in their Miss Teenage Hairspray official dance-off!"

It was the most important part of the show. Each of the girls would get to do a solo dance. The switchboard would stay open so people could call in last-minute votes. When the dances ended, Miss Teenage Hairspray would be crowned.

The music began and Lou Ann stepped forward first.

Now it was time to put Tracy's plan into action.

Tracy boldly walked right up to the main entrance to the TV station. The police officers spotted her right away.

"Confirmed sighting," the chief reported to Velma.

The officers swarmed Tracy, grabbing her. Tracy smiled. But it wasn't Tracy at all.

It was Wilbur in disguise!

"Looking for someone?" Wilbur asked in a high voice.

The police had no idea they didn't have the real Tracy and dragged Wilbur toward the doors of the station.

Inside the building, a group of janitors locked all the doors from the inside. They used heavy chains and locks. But they weren't janitors at all. Seaweed, Penny, and their friends had sneaked into WYZT, dressed up like janitors.

The police officers tried to open the doors to bring Tracy inside to Velma. But none of the doors would open, thanks to the "janitors."

Wilbur grinned. "Aw, they never like to seat you after the show starts."

The police quickly realized that they had been duped, and the chief reported the bad news to Velma.

"What?" Velma asked furiously. "Please, these people aren't capable of a diversion. That's beyond their mental capability." Then a thought struck her. "Oh no. What if she's already in the building? What if she's been in here for hours? And you've locked yourselves out. Morons!"

Velma ran off in a panic. The chief knew they had to find a way inside—and fast!

"Break down the door!" he ordered his men.

The officers grabbed the nearest, biggest thing they could find—the giant can of Ultra-Clutch Hairspray. They used it like a battering ram, pounding it into the door.

While the cops were distracted, Wilbur quietly walked away. When he knocked on the building's side door, Seaweed let him in with a smile.

"Those guys are a couple doughnuts short of a deck," Wilbur said, shaking his head.

Back onstage, Amber finished her dance and the crowd burst into applause. The scoreboard now showed that Amber had a big lead over Tracy.

Corny frowned sadly. He really didn't want to see Amber win.

"Well that seems to be . . . the last of our contestants," Corny said, but his voice wasn't as perky as usual. "Except for the one who's at large."

"At *very* large!" Amber said, laughing at her own joke. Then she stopped abruptly. "Announce the winner!"

Corny tapped his foot. He wished there was some way he could stall . . .

The crowd clapped. They wanted to see a winner, too.

"All right, all right," Corny sighed. "We're moments away from the final tally."

Velma stormed toward the front door. The police had finally managed to push it open. The men leaned against the walls, exhausted.

"What is with you people?" she asked. "I mean, how hard is it to beat down a door?"

"That hairspray battering ram was heavy," the chief told her.

Velma froze at the word "heavy." She ran over to the can and saw that there was a little door in the back

. . . and that it was open.

"You idiots! You brought her inside the building!" Velma shouted.

Back on the stage, Corny couldn't put it off any longer. He had to announce the winner.

Music swelled as a cool silver throne shaped like a rocket ship descended from the ceiling. When it landed, Miss Teenage Hairspray 1962 would climb onboard.

"It is my . . ." Corny began. His voice faltered. " . . . obligation, to announce that Amber Von Tussle . . ."

Suddenly, the doors to the rocket ship opened up.

Tracy stood inside!

" . . . is about to get outdanced!" Tracy cried.

16

The crowd cheered as Tracy stepped out of the rocket. She wore a sequined black-and-white minidress that glittered under the lights. Her streaked brown hair had been ironed flat. Tracy was ready to show off her new attitude—and her new hair that went with it.

Tracy started dancing across the floor in her white go-go boots. She sang a song she'd been practicing all night.

> *"You can't stop an avalanche as it races down the hill.*
>
> *You can try to stop the seasons, girl, but you know you never will.*
>
> *And you can try to stop my dancing feet, but I just cannot stand still!*
>
> *'Cause the world keeps spinning round and round.*
>
> *And my heart's keeping time to the speed of sound.*

*I was lost till I heard the drums then I found
my way!*

'Cause you can't stop the beat!"

Link ran up to Tracy, a huge smile on his face. He joined in the song.

*"'Cause you can't stop the motion of the
ocean or the sun in the sky.*

*You can wonder if you wanna but I never
ask why.*

*And if you try to hold me down I'm gonna
spit in your eye and say*

That you can't stop the beat!"

Velma could hear Tracy singing onstage, but she couldn't get back inside the TV studio. All the studio doors were locked from the inside, too.

Onstage, Amber lunged at the throne. She stood on it and stomped her foot.

"It's mine! That throne's mine!" she yelled.

In the rafters above, Seaweed and Penny nodded at each other. They began to hoist up the ropes of the rocket ship. Amber grabbed the sides of the throne as it hovered over the stage.

The Hollywood agents stared at the scene, not sure what to make of it.

"They love you, Link!" Tracy assured him.

Link grinned. "Not after this . . ."

He winked at the agents. Then he pulled Little Inez out onstage.

Little Inez grinned at Link and began to dance. When Link danced with Little Inez, Tracy beamed with pride. Not only was Link standing up for what he knew was right—that boy had finally found his groove!

"Ladies and gentlemen, Miss Little Inez Stubbs!" Corny announced.

The audience cheered. This little girl could really dance!

In the WYZT newsroom, the anchorman saw the scene on the TV monitor behind him. He dutifully reported the news story.

"And this is live at WYZT, where the Miss Teenage Hairspray pageant has been disrupted by the surprise entry of fugitive Tracy Turnblad, whose imminent arrest we should be seeing in just a few moments . . . or maybe a few bars." The anchorman bopped in his

seat. Could Tracy Turnblad be all that bad?

Penny and Seaweed sang along from the side of the stage. They had discarded their janitor disguises. For the first time in her life, Penny wore a pretty flowered dress. Her blond hair fell in curls down her back. She even had on heels.

Seaweed grabbed Penny's hand and pulled her out onstage. Penny was shy, but her love for Seaweed made her strong. She started to sing.

> *"You can't stop a river as it rushes to the sea.*
> *You can try to stop the hands of time, but you know it just can't be.*
> *And if they try to stop us, Seaweed, I'll call the NAACP!"*

Seaweed sang with her.

> *"'Cause the world keeps spinning round and round,*
> *And my heart's keeping time to the speed of sound.*
> *I was lost till I heard the drums then I found my way.*
> *'Cause you can't stop the beat!"*

All of Baltimore watched as Seaweed danced with Penny, and Link danced with Little Inez. TV reporters from all over the city flocked outside the studio building.

"That's right, Steve," one reporter announced. "Interracial dancing has broken out on the WYZT stage!"

Seaweed and Penny celebrated their triumph with a kiss.

The news spread fast all over the city. Some people were upset. But most people were excited. Just like Tracy and her friends, they were ready for things to change. People from all over town began calling the studio. The phones rang like crazy.

The crowd inside the TV studio clapped along to the beat. Above them, Amber desperately tried to keep her grip on the throne. But her hands slipped, and she dropped to the stage.

Corny shrugged into the camera. "Live television! There's nothing like it."

Out in the hallway, the police officers finally broke down the studio door. They began to rush to arrest

Tracy, but Velma stopped them.

"Wait until we go to commercial," she told them. As much as she hated to admit it, she knew her viewers liked Tracy. She didn't want to look bad on TV.

"And, it's the moment you've all been screaming for!" Corny announced, as the music faded. "As you know, we've kept the lines open up to the last minute. And those lines have been burning up our switchboard. Never in the history of this pageant has there been such a surge of late voting!"

Tracy and Amber stood side by side, waiting for the results. The girl at the scoreboard walked up and handed Corny an envelope and the Miss Teenage Hairspray crown.

"Baltimore, you have picked a winner," he said. He opened the envelope and walked toward Tracy. "And our new Miss Teenage Hairspray is . . . Inez Stubbs!"

Corny walked past Tracy and put the crown on Little Inez's head. Tracy was shocked at first, but then she screamed with joy. Link screamed with her.

Inez did what every beauty pageant winner does— she burst into tears of happiness.

Velma stormed out onto the stage. "What?" she shouted. "She's not even a candidate. I want these people arrested."

Velma suddenly realized she was on camera. She smiled nervously into the lens.

"Ever heard of a write-in?" Corny asked.

"No! This is invalid!" Velma fumed. "I demand—"

Corny pulled the contest rules from his jacket pocket. "Anyone who dances for it is eligible," he informed her. "Rule thirty, paragraph five, asterisk, down at the bottom."

Corny looked down at Inez, beaming. "This also makes you the lead dancer of *The Corny Collins Show*. *The Corny Collins Show* is now and forever officially integrated!"

Everyone in the crowd rose to their feet, clapping. Maybelle walked out onstage, followed by the kids from the record shop. Tracy gave Link a big hug.

"We did it!" she cried.

Velma screamed and ran off the stage, pulling Amber with her.

120

17

For the first time in history, blacks and whites appeared onstage together on Baltimore TV. They celebrated their victory the best way they knew how.

They danced!

> "*Ever since we first saw the light,*
> *A man and woman liked to shake it on a Saturday night.*
> *And so I'm gonna shake and shimmy it with all of my might today.*
> *'Cause you can't stop*
> *The motion of the ocean or the rain from above.*
> *You can try to stop the paradise we're dreaming of*
> *But you cannot stop the rhythm of two hearts in love to stay!*"

Backstage, Amber's toes tapped to the music.

"Stop that at once!" Velma yelled.

"I lost, Mom," Amber said. "Let's just deal with it."

"You did not lose!" Velma shrieked. "I know for a FACT that you did not lose, because I switched the tally myself!"

Velma suddenly got an uncomfortable feeling. She turned to see the camera pointed directly at her and Amber. Behind the grinning cameraman stood Edna and Wilbur.

"Smile, Miss Crabmeat!" Edna said.

"I thought that was a very good shot," Wilbur added.

Velma's shocked face appeared on television screens all over the city. Panicked, she tried to push the cameraman away. "Get that away from me! What are you doing? Go to commercial. Go. GO!"

The cameraman didn't budge. Mr. Spritzer walked up beside him.

"Velma," he said sternly.

"No," Velma said weakly. "Don't."

"Pack your desk," he said. "You have tainted the name of Ultra-Clutch. You're fired."

"How do you taint a cancerous can of chemicals?" Velma snapped. "I can't be fired!"

She rushed out onstage, her eyes wild.

Edna followed her. She shook her booty along with the dancers. Then she joined the song, too.

> "*You can't stop my happiness 'cause I like the way I am.*
>
> *And you can't stop my knife and fork when I see a Christmas ham.*
>
> *So if you don't like the way I look, well, I just don't give a darn!*
>
> *'Cause the world keeps spinning round and round,*
>
> *And my heart's keeping time to the speed of sound.*
>
> *I was lost till I heard the drums then I found my way.*
>
> *'Cause you can't stop the beat!*"

Tracy and Inez ran up and danced with Edna. Edna launched into the Twist, the Pony, the Mashed Potato—every dance she'd ever seen Tracy do in their living room. The audience screamed in approval.

Velma didn't care about waiting for a commercial break anymore. She led the police chief and his officers onstage. Corny, Link, Penny, and Seaweed stood between Tracy and the police.

"Corny, do something!" Velma pleaded. "This show is turning to gumbo."

"This is the future, Velma," Corny told her. "Maybelle, get down there! This is your time."

Maybelle took the stage in a glamorous gold gown and red feather boa. Her voice rocked the studio.

> "Oh, oh, oh, you can't stop today as it comes speeding down the track.
>
> Child, yesterday is history and it's never coming back.
>
> 'Cause tomorrow is a brand-new day and it don't know white from black!
>
> 'Cause the world keeps spinning round and round,
>
> And my heart's keeping time to the speed of sound.
>
> I was lost till I heard the drums, then I found my way.

'Cause you can't stop the beat!"

Corny turned to the police chief. "Aren't you kind of arresting the wrong person?" he asked.

Everyone on the stage turned around and pointed at Velma.

"*Lock up the Von Tussles. Come on shake your fanny muscles!*" they sang.

"*No, I can't!*" sang the chief.

"*Yes, you can!*"

"*No, I can't!*" sang the chief.

"*Yes, you can. Yes, you can!*"

The chief got caught up in the happy energy of the song.

"*Yes, I can!*" he belted out. He tore up the warrant, then he motioned to his officers. They handcuffed Velma and led her away.

A wave of joy cascaded over the studio. Everyone sang together now.

"*Ever since we first saw the sun,*
A man and woman liked to shake it when
the day is done.
And so I'm gonna shake and shimmy

Now and have some fun today.

'Cause you can't stop the beat!"

"The motion of the ocean or the rain from above," sang Tracy and Link.

"They can try to stop the paradise we're dreaming of," sang Penny and Seaweed.

"But you cannot stop the rhythm of two hearts in love to stay!" sang Maybelle.

"You can't stop the beat!

You can't stop the beat!

You can't stop the beat!"

Tracy danced into Link's arms. She looked into his blue eyes as he bent down to kiss her.

The last beats of the music faded away.

But the song in Tracy's heart was just beginning.